```
JE                                  Copy 1
Bro

          Brockel, Ray
      Rodney bounced too much on
               Monday




         GRANVILLE PUBLIC LIBRARY
            GRANVILLE, OHIO
```

RODNEY
BOUNCED
TOO MUCH
ON MONDAY

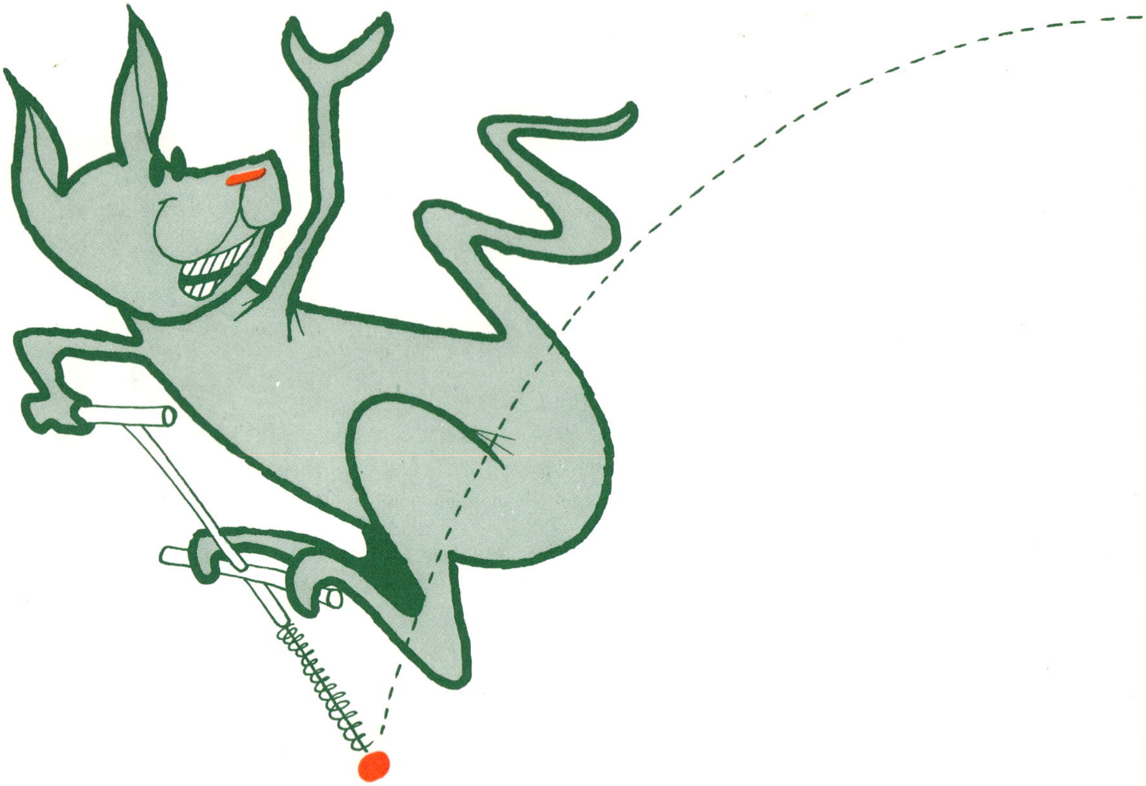

Illustrated by

Joe Reisner

RODNEY BOUNCED TOO MUCH ON MONDAY

by

Ray Broekel

GRANVILLE PUBLIC LIBRARY
GRANVILLE, OHIO

E. C. Seale & Company, Inc.
INDIANAPOLIS

Library of Congress Catalog Card No. 64-15741

Copyright © 1964 by E. C. Seale & Company, Inc.
All rights reserved
Printed in the United States of America

All of the animals in the Pecksmith Zoo were near the front gate.
Today was "RODNEY" Day at the Zoo.
Rodney was a kangaroo.
He was coming to the Pecksmith Zoo all the way from Australia.

The Murphy Marching Band was lined up on one side of the main gate. The band was ready to play the minute Rodney arrived.

The Pecksmith Zoo Quartette was lined up on the other side of the main gate. The Quartette was ready to sing the minute Rodney arrived.

"When is Rodney coming?" asked the polar bear.
"When is Rodney coming?"
He had already asked this same question a thousand times.

"As soon as he gets here," said the keeper for the thousandth time.

The Zoo Quartette began to sing, but no one could hear them. The Band was playing too loudly. It probably was just as well that the Band was playing too loudly as the Quartette hadn't practiced singing all week.

The truck pulled to a stop.
Out popped Rodney!
Out he popped, bouncing on a pogo stick.
BOI-ING!
BOI-ING!
BOI-ING! — he bounced.

From the minute he arrived at the
Pecksmith Zoo, Rodney never stopped bouncing.
Not even for breakfast,
not even for lunch,
not even for dinner.

For breakfast he caught pieces of toast that popped out of a toaster—as he bounced.

For lunch he made cheese sandwiches—as he bounced.

For dinner he had ice cream sundaes—as he bounced.

The first few months the other animals in the zoo didn't mind Rodney's bouncing. But then, one Monday, Rodney began bouncing in the wrong places.

That Monday the hippo was brushing his teeth. Rodney bounced on the tip of the hippo's nose with his pogo stick.
BOI-ING!

20

Toothpaste went squishing all over the hippo's face.

That Monday the pelican was polishing his beak.
Rodney bounced on the tip of the pelican's beak.
BOI-ING!

The pelican did three quick somersaults and landed in a big bowl of mashed potatoes.

That Monday the polar bear was cooling off in his pool.
Rodney bounced into the pool.
BOI-ING!
SPLASH!
All the water flew out of the pool.

That Monday the giraffe was hanging out the washing.
Rodney bounced down the giraffe's neck.
BOI-ING!
Clothes went flying; clothespins went flying—
all over the place.

That Monday the laughing hyena was brushing his tail.
Rodney bounced on the laughing hyena's tail.
BOI-ING!
The hyena, who usually laughed, that Monday said, "Ouch!"

That Monday the crocodile was sunning himself.
He was holding a book and a pair of sunglasses.
Rodney bounced in the middle of the crocodile's stomach.
BOI-ING!
Up shot the sunglasses — and the book.

"Oh, for goodness sakes," said the keeper.
"What are we going to do with that crazy kangaroo on the pogo stick?"

"Let's have a meeting in the Pecksmith Zoo Town Hall," screamed the hyena.
"Yes!" yelled the giraffe.
"Yes!" bellowed the crocodile.

"The meeting will come to order," said the keeper.
Just then Rodney bounced through a window.
He landed on the table — BOI-ING! — right on
top of a bottle of ink.
Then he bounced out through another window.

"Send him back to Australia where he came from," shouted the polar bear.

"Make him clean all the windows of the Empire State Building," shouted the hippo.

"Make him pick rotten apples off the tops of tall apple trees," shouted the pelican.

The keeper pounded for order.
"Let's hear what Zanzibar has to say," he said.
(Whenever the zoo animals had a problem, they asked Zanzibar for advice.)

Zanzibar said, "Does anyone have a Friend-in-the-Big-City?"
Sid, the zebra, was sitting in the front row.
Sid said, "I have a Friend-in-the-Big-City."

"Phone your friend," said Zanzibar.
"Tell him to come out to the Pecksmith Zoo.
Tell him Rodney is just what he needs."

Sid picked up the telephone.
"Operator, get me my Friend-in-the-Big-City."

"Hello, hello? Friend-in-the-Big-City?
This is Sid. Can you come out to the Pecksmith Zoo
right away? We have something to show you."

Before you could say
"Mecklin von Lichtenstein"
　　　　or
"Franzel Schnitzelspiel"
(both of which are pretty hard to say
　　　unless you know German),
the Friend-from-the-Big-City was at the
Pecksmith Zoo Town Hall.

"What do you have to show me, Sid?" he asked.

Just then Rodney bounced through the window.
He landed on the head of the Friend-from-the-Big-City.
BOI-ING!
Rodney bounced out again.

"What do you think, Friend-from-the-Big-City?" asked Sid.

"Wonderful, wonderful!" shouted the Friend-from-the-Big-City. "He's just what I need. I can put him to work right away if you can just get him to bounce over to the Big City."

"I'll see what I can do," said Sid. "But first I will need a pogo stick."

42

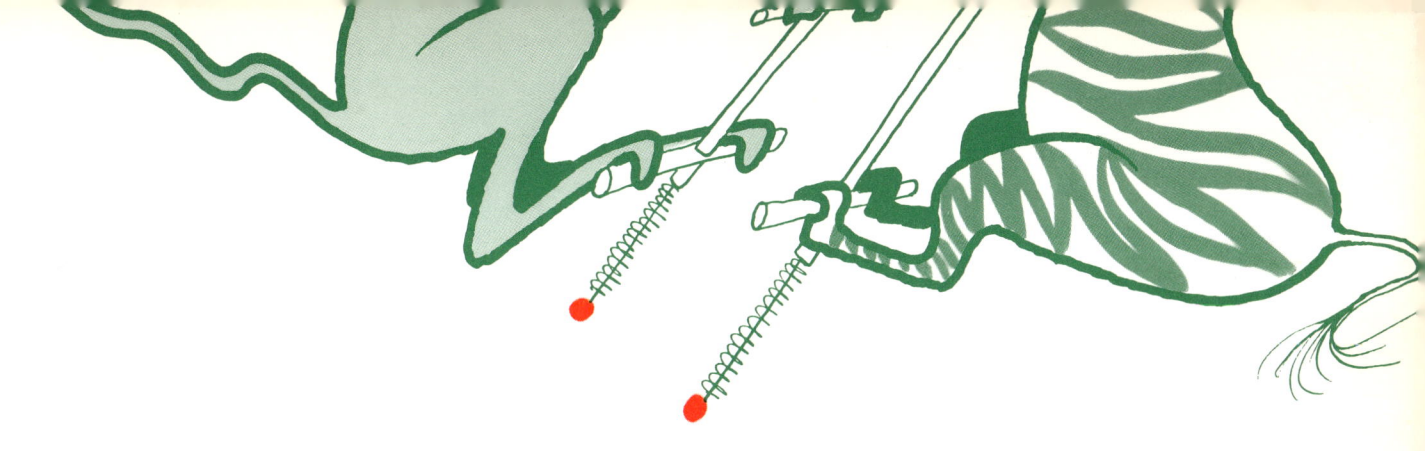

Sid got a pogo stick and bounced up and down with Rodney so the two of them could talk.

When they were near the ground, the other animals could hear them as they mumbled together.

When they were high off the ground, the other animals couldn't hear them as they mumbled together.

Pretty soon Rodney and Sid were bouncing off toward the Big City.

CLAUDIA'S TOY SHOP

LIZ's dresses

45

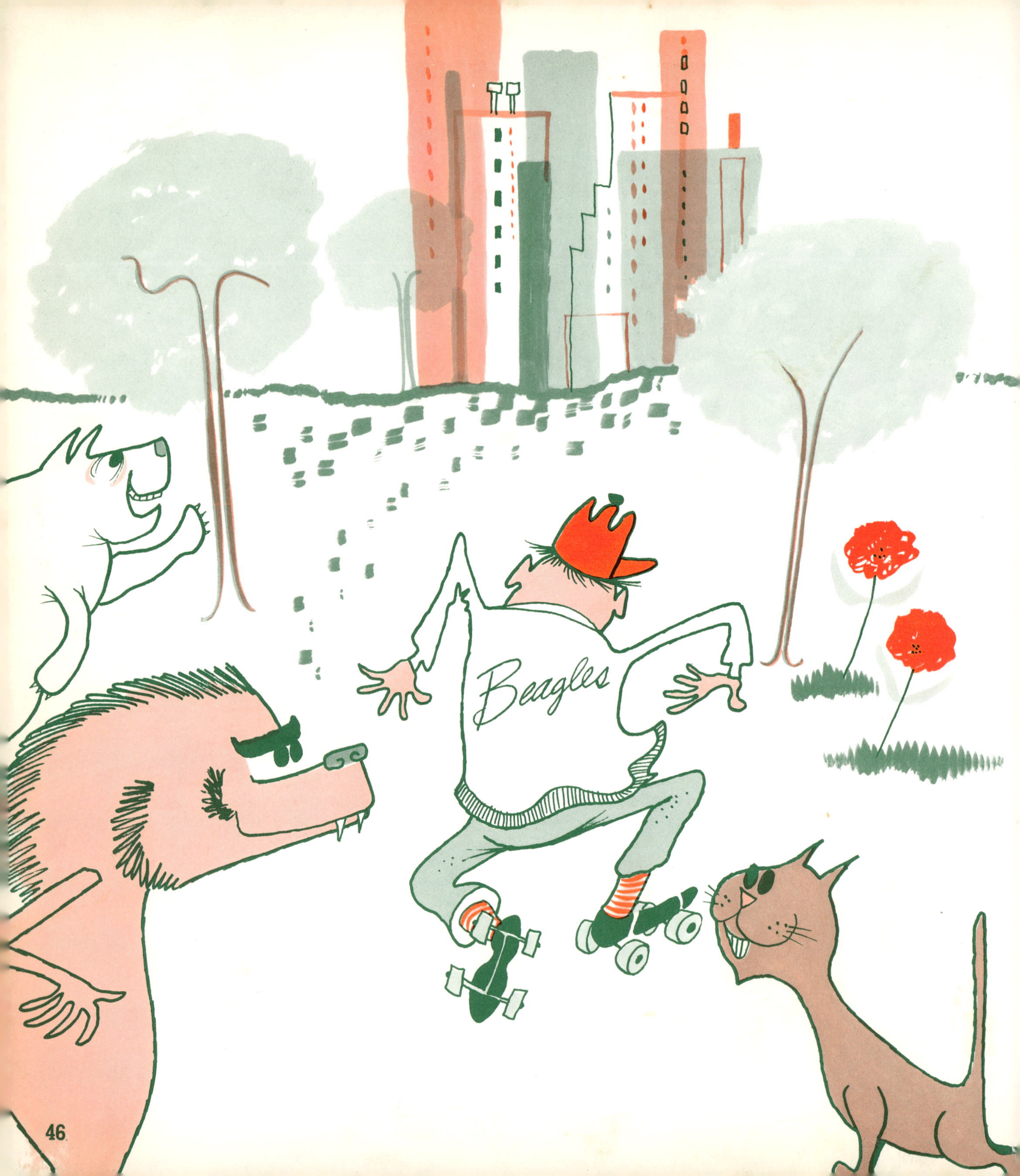
Beagles

Sid's Friend-from-the-Big-City borrowed a pair
of roller skates from the keeper and skated after them.
The Pecksmith Zoo Animals gave three loud cheers.
Rodney was leaving the zoo.
Rodney would no longer bother them.

One week later a telegram arrived at the Pecksmith Zoo.

The telegram was from Sid.
The keeper opened the telegram.
The keeper read the telegram to himself.
Then the keeper read the telegram aloud:

"Friends at the Pecksmith Zoo:
  Come to the Big City.
  Come to see what Rodney is doing.
  Rodney is famous."

So all the animals went to the Big City.

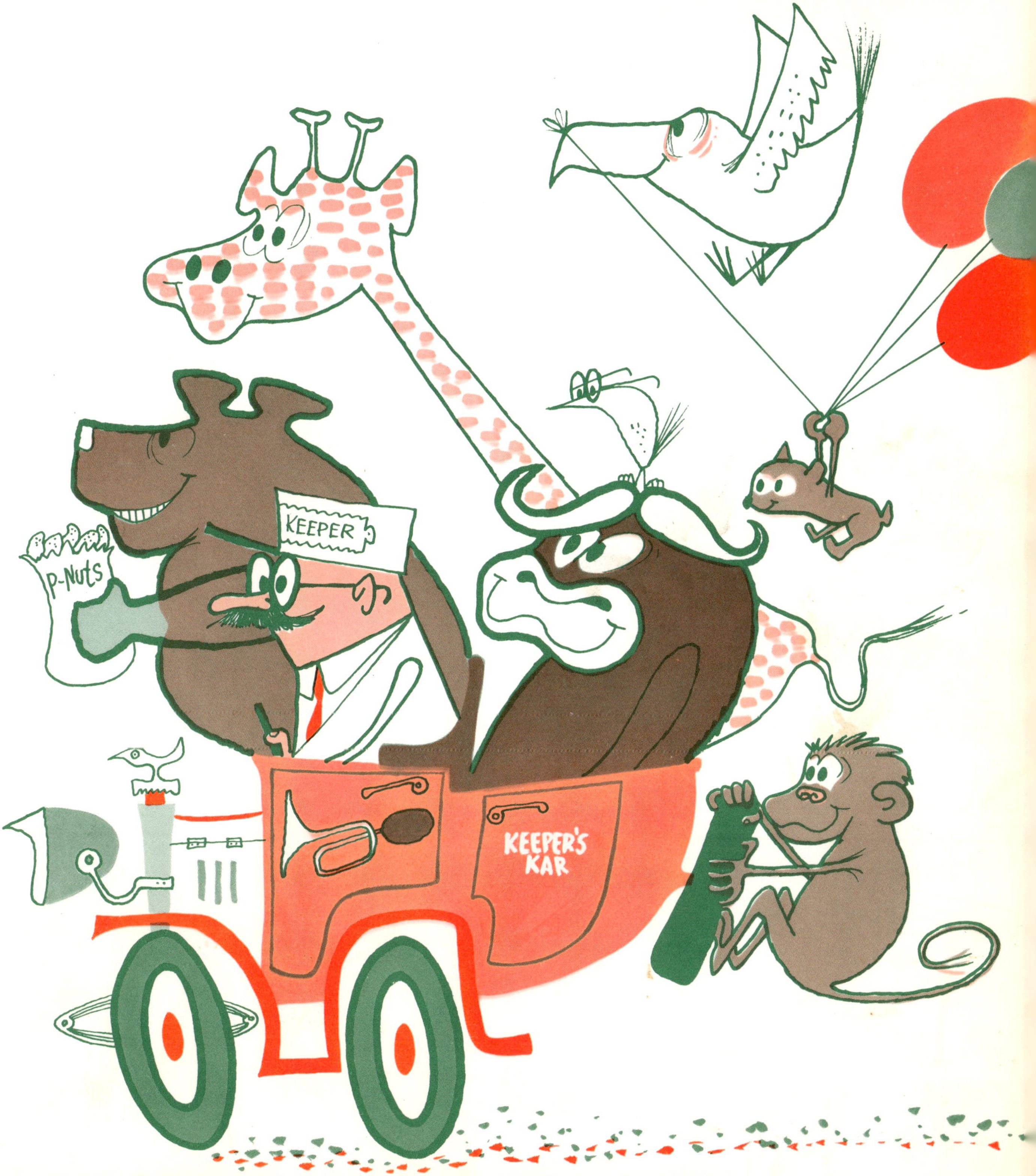
KEEPER
P-NUTS
KEEPER'S KAR

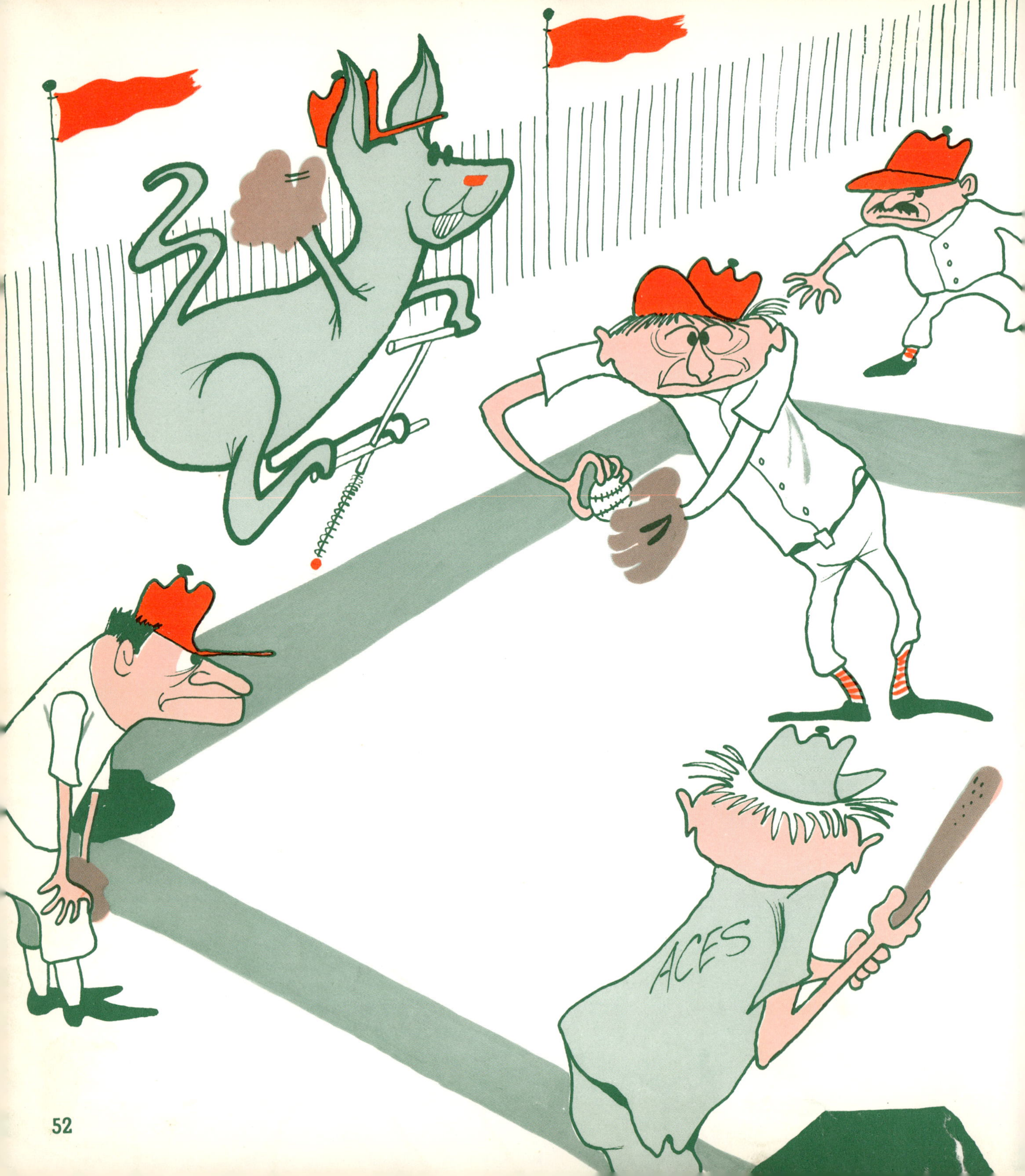
ACES

Where did they go in the Big City?
They went to see Sid's friend.
Sid's friend was the manager of a baseball team.
The animals went out to the baseball park.
They watched Rodney play in a baseball game.

Rodney bounced around the baseball field on his pogo stick.
He caught every ball hit by the other team.
Rodney's team was winning.
RODNEY WAS FAMOUS!

After the game Rodney autographed baseballs.
He gave a baseball to each of the Pecksmith Zoo Animals.

From the top of his pogo stick, Rodney waved goodbye to the animals as they left the baseball park.

When the animals got back to the Pecksmith Zoo,
Sid painted some signs.

He put one of the signs on the hippo's nose.

He stuck one in the polar bear's pool.

He hung one from the pelican's beak.

He hung one from the giraffe's clothesline.

He stuck one on the crocodile's stomach.

And if you'll look closely,
you'll even see a very small sign that he put
on the laughing hyena's tail.
What did Sid's signs say?
They said,
"RODNEY, MY FAMOUS FRIEND,
    BOUNCED
        HERE!"